Weekly Reader Books presents

This

READ with ME

Book
Belongs To

_____

Library of Congress Cataloging in Publication Data

Horowitz, Susan.
   Little Red Riding Hood with Benjy and Bubbles.
   (Read with me series)
   SUMMARY: A rhymed retelling of the classic tale with Benjy the bunny and Bubbles the cat clarifying values as the story unfolds.
   [1. Fairy tales. 2. Folklore—France. 3. Stories in rhyme] I. Perle, Ruth Lerner, joint author. II. Maestro, Giulio.
III. Title. IV. Series.
           PZ8.3H785Li   [398.2]   [E]   78-55627
                ISBN 0-03-044961-8

           Weekly Reader Books' edition

Little Red Riding Hood

with Benjy and Bubbles

Adapted by **SUSAN HOROWITZ**
and **RUTH LERNER PERLE**

Illustrated by **GIULIO MAESTRO**

Holt, Rinehart and Winston • New York

There once was a girl who wore on her head,
A velvet hood of scarlet red.
The hood was made by her Grandmother,
So she never dressed in any other.
And everyone who knew her, would
Call her Little Red Riding Hood.

A little girl had a red hood.
Her name was Little Red Riding Hood.

One day her mother said, "Please take
This basket of bread, fruit and cake
To Grandmother, who has a chill
And lies in bed alone and ill.

"Hurry now, and don't delay—
And stop for nothing on the way.
Take Benjy the bunny along to guide you
And see that he remains beside you."

Her mother said, "Grandmother is sick.
Please take this food to her house.
Do not stop on the way."

They were not long upon their way,
When they heard a deep voice say,
"How nice to see you here today!"

Red Riding Hood, to her surprise,
Saw a wolf with yellow eyes.
He had large ears, enormous paws,
And pointed teeth were in his jaws.

The girl, not knowing what to do,
Politely said, "Good day to you."
And from a tree, high on a bough,
Bubbles the cat replied, "Meow."

A Wolf said, "Good day, Red Riding Hood."

The Wolf winked up at the grinning cat,
Then turned to the girl and started to chat.
"What's in your basket?" asked the beast.
The girl said, "Mother made a feast
Of fruits and honey cake and bread
For Grandmother, who's sick in bed.
She is expecting me today,
So I had best be on my way."

Little Red Riding Hood said,
"I am going to Grandmother's house.
I must not stop on the way."

The Wolf decided to pretend
To be Red Riding Hood's good friend.
He smiled and said, "Don't run away!
Why don't you stop a bit and play?
The birds are singing in their bowers,
And look at all the pretty flowers!"
But he determined, as he smiled,
To eat both Grandmother and child.
(And Bubbles made her private goal—
A tasty rabbit casserole.)

"You must stop to pick flowers!"
said the Wolf.

Benjy the bunny twitched an ear
As if to say, "Please don't stop here!"
But Riding Hood looked all around—
The air was filled with songbirds' sound;
And violets and daffodils
Were blooming up and down the hills.
She said, "These flowers are so gay,
I'll stop to pick a big bouquet.
It should take at most an hour,
And Grandmother will love the flowers!"

And so, Little Red Riding Hood
Skipped carelessly into the wood.
And the Wolf, pleased with his awful plot,
Raced off with Bubbles as quick as a shot!

Red Riding Hood stopped to
pick flowers.
The Wolf ran to Grandmother's house.

They ran and ran and ran some more
To Grandmother's house and knocked on the door.

Inside, Grandmother was taking a nap,
Wearing her nightgown and lacy nightcap.
When she heard knocking, she sat up in bed,
Adjusted her glasses and cheerfully said,
"Red Riding Hood, is that *you* I hear?"
And the Wolf said, "Yes, Grandmother, dear!"
"I've been waiting for you!" the old woman cried.
"Lift up the latch and come right inside."

The Wolf tapped on Grandmother's door.
He said he was Red Riding Hood.
Grandmother said, "Come in!"

The Wolf crashed in with an evil leer—
Grandmother cried, "HELP!" but no one could hear!
Toward the dear woman, that mean old Wolf sped,
Swallowed her whole and then jumped into bed!
He dressed in her nightgown and lacy nightcap,
Then lay down on the bed for an after-meal nap.

And Bubbles, without a meow or a purr,
Curled up in a corner and licked at her fur.

The Wolf ate Grandmother in a gulp.
He put on her cap and gown.
Then he jumped into bed.

Meanwhile, in a meadow, deep in the wood,
Gathering flowers, was Red Riding Hood.
Each flower she picked seemed more fine than the last
And swiftly and sweetly, the afternoon passed.

At last, Benjy showed her the darkening sky,
And Riding Hood realized the day had gone by.
"Oh Benjy!" she cried. "It's gotten so late—
Let's run all the way to Grandmother's gate."

When they arrived, Red Riding Hood spied—
The latch, all unfastened; the door, open wide!

It was late! Red Riding Hood ran
to Grandmother's house.

She rushed in the house and up to the bed,
Where the Wolf lay disguised, nightcap on his head.
Red Riding Hood cried, "Grandma, you look strange!"
And the Wolf said, "My dear, sometimes people change."
The girl cried, "Grandmother, I see a large ear!"
The Wolf said, "At my age, it helps me to hear."
"But Grandma," the girl cried, "your eyes are big, too!"
The Wolf said, "I grew them for looking at you."
"But Grandma," she cried, "what large paws,
                                    —I mean fingers!"
The Wolf said, "They'll give you a love pat that lingers!"

Grandmother looked strange.

"What big ears you have!" said Red Riding Hood.

"The better to hear you," said the Wolf.

"What big eyes you have!" she said.

"The better to see you," said the Wolf.

"What big hands you have!" she said.

"The better to hug you," said the Wolf.

"But Grandma," she cried, "your teeth are so pointed,
And your mouth is so wide—it looks double-jointed!"
"That's true," said the Wolf, "you have excellent sight.
Now watch as I swallow you up in one bite!"

"What big teeth you have!"
said Red Riding Hood.
"The better to eat you!" said the Wolf.

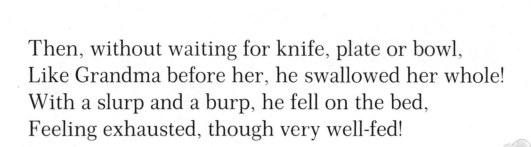

Then, without waiting for knife, plate or bowl,
Like Grandma before her, he swallowed her whole!
With a slurp and a burp, he fell on the bed,
Feeling exhausted, though very well-fed!

He lay on his back and started to snore
As Benjy the bunny ran out the door.

The Wolf ate Red Riding Hood in a gulp.
Then he fell asleep.

The snores of the Wolf were so loud and so strong,
That a woodsman, out walking, sensed something
was wrong.
"I'd better look into this matter," he said.
So he entered and found the old Wolf on the bed.
He thought to himself, "This Wolf looks suspicious—
He seems to have swallowed something delicious!"

He looked all around—Grandmother was missing!
And under the bed, he heard a cat hissing.

And so, to clear up any lingering doubt,
He slit open the Wolf—and what tumbled out?
Grandmother! And with no further delay,
Red Riding Hood popped out the very same way.

A man came in.
He set Grandmother and
Red Riding Hood free.

The woman, the child and the woodsman embraced,
Then agreed on a plan in the greatest of haste.
They filled up the Wolf from his toes to his head
With great heavy stones to be sure he was dead.

"Now," Grandmother said, "let us share a fine meal,
We all have been through an awful ordeal."
Benjy the bunny stood on his hind feet
And Red Riding Hood gave him a carrot to eat.
Then Bubbles ran in and ran out again
And hasn't been seen at Grandma's since then.

Red Riding Hood's life from then on after,
Was filled with joy and love and laughter.

Now the Wolf was dead.
Red Riding Hood and Grandmother
were happy.

THE END